BAT*napped!*

Sharon Jennings

HIP-JR.

HIP Junior
Copyright © 2008 by Sharon Jennings

LIBRARY AND ARCHIVES CANADA CATALOGUING IN PUBLICATION

Jennings, Sharon
    Batnapped / Sharon Jennings.

(HIP jr)
ISBN 978-1-897039-30-4

    I. Title. II. Series
PS8569.E563B36 2008   jC813'.54   C2008-902049-9

General editor: Paul Kropp
Text design and typesetting: Laura Brady
Illustrations drawn by: Kalle Malloy
Cover design: Robert Corrigan

2 3 4 5 6 7   11 10 09 08

Printed and bound in Canada

High Interest Publishing is an imprint of the
Chestnut Publishing Group

Valentine's Day brings trouble to the Bat Gang. Sam gets tickets to a Leafs game. But Simon would rather go to the school dance – with a girl! And then things get worse. Sam and the girl both get kidnapped!

CHAPTER ONE

Dumped!

My best friend is a weenie.

That's right. You heard me. Simon is a weenie. A reject. A loser. I could go on.

You want to know why? I'll tell you why. You'd better sit down. This isn't pretty.

Last week, my dad scored two tickets – two *platinum* tickets – to the Leafs hockey game for Friday night. Right at center ice. But my dad couldn't go. So he gave the tickets to me. "Take Simon," he said. Well, duh. Simon is my best buddy. So I hopped

3

the fences to Simon's backyard and ran into the kitchen.

"Simon!" I yelled. "Look what I've got!" And I waved the tickets under his nose.

Simon took one look and said, "Wow! Who you going with?" And I said, "Are you an idiot? You, stupid." That's when he said, "Oh, I can't go. I'm ... uh ... er ... well ..." And he looked up at the ceiling. And he looked down at the floor. And he looked at the cupboards, the fridge, the stove. He looked like one of those bobble-head dolls.

"What's going on?" I asked, grabbing him by the ears.

So Simon, he got all red, and then he said, "I'm busy, Sam. I'm ... uh ... er ... well ..."

So I shook his head and said, "What is it?!"

And then he told me, "I'm taking Carla to the school dance. For Valentine's."

I stared at him. "You're kidding, right?"

He shook his head.

"You'd give up Leafs tickets, center ice, for a girl?"

He nodded.

"Are you sick? She's a *girl*."

Simon smiled like a moron. "I know she's a *girl*. I kind of like her."

"I'm going to barf," I said.

So now you know. Now you know why Simon is a weenie.

But it got worse. Simon began eating his lunch with Carla. He walked home with Carla. He did his homework with Carla. He watched TV with Carla.

One day I followed them home. I walked behind them all the way, making kissing noises.

Carla turned around and said, "Sam Fletcher! You are *so* immature!"

"*I'm* immature?! I'm not the one wearing that stupid hat." I pointed to Carla's head. She had on this pink hat with hearts hanging off it. "Isn't that right, Simon? Isn't that a stupid hat?"

"I gave her that hat, Sam," replied Simon.

Whaaaat?!

"Yeah," said Carla. "It's a Valentine present, so there, moron."

"Who are you calling a moron?" I demanded. "Come on, Simon. Carla is insulting your best friend! Say something. Tell her off!"

But Simon looked at me and said, "Go home, Sam. I'm busy."

Whaaaat?

So I stomped off. Then I turned and yelled "*Rusil*!"

Rusil is Bat code for "loser." Simon and I have been writing and talking in Bat code ever since we were little kids. We called ourselves the Bat Gang. Of course, there are only two members in the Bat Gang, so we're not much of a gang. But you get the idea.

Anyhow, I threw a snowball at Simon. I swear, I really was aiming for Simon. But I missed. I hit Carla instead, on her hat. She fell down.

Simon helped her up and then took off after me. I didn't expect him to be so angry. I thought it was kind of funny. Simon grabbed me and punched me and knocked me down. Then he pushed my face into the snow.

"Get lost, jerk!" he yelled. "Hear me, Sam? Leave me alone from now on!"

What a weenie. "Yeah, four eyes, I hear you."

But it still got worse.

I got home and my dad was on the phone. He gave me a real funny look and I got a real funny feeling. An "uh-oh" kind of feeling.

"Yes, Mrs. Tutti. I understand, Mrs. Tutti. Of course, Mrs. Tutti."

Uh-oh. Mrs. Tutti is Carla's mom.

"Of course I'll speak to Sam, Mrs. Tutti," my dad went on. "Don't you worry, Mrs. Tutti. I'll deal with him." Another funny look from my dad. I tried to sneak away, but my dad hung up the phone and yelled, "Get back here, Sam!"

"I can explain," I said. "It was an accident. I meant to hit Simon." And I told him all about Simon dumping me for a girl.

"A *girl*, Dad. I mean – gross!"

My dad just sighed and rolled his eyes. "Your mother is a *girl*, Sam!"

"No she's not!" I yelled. Well, I mean she is, but

that's different.

"So here's the deal, Sam," said my dad. "You have to apologize to Carla. And I have a week to think about giving you those hockey tickets. Or not."

Whaaaat?!

"No fair!" I yelled. But then I stopped. What was the use?

And it still got worse.

I usually hang out with Simon Friday nights, but he was busy with Carla. So I went downstairs to watch a movie. *Death by Zombies* was on – one of the greatest movies of all time. But my little sister, Ellen, was watching the big-screen TV already.

"Beat it," I told her.

"Beat it yourself," she replied. "It's my turn to watch TV. And I'm watching *Cinderella*."

So I sat down and watched *Cinderella* with my little sister on a Friday night.

What a weenie!

CHAPTER TWO

Sucking It Up

On Monday morning, I knew what I had to do. I didn't want to do it, but I wanted those hockey tickets.

I had to apologize to Carla. Then I started this debate in my head.

Apologize! I'd rather die.

Hockey tickets. . . .

Be a man, I told myself.

Suck it up, I told myself

Step up to the plate, I told myself.

Take one for the team, I told myself.

So I waited in the schoolyard until I saw Carla come through the gate. She went over to her group of stupid friends. All the girls started talking. Then someone turned and she pointed at me. They all started laughing.

Be a man, I told myself.

Suck it up, I told myself.

Oh, just get it over with, moron, I told myself.

So I marched over to the girls. I was going to apologize. Really, I was. But, I don't know how it happened, just as I got close, I slipped on some ice. My legs went right out from under me. Then I started sliding. I slid along until I banged into Carla and knocked her down.

Carla started crying. Then all the other girls started screaming. And our teacher, Mr. Chong, ran over and tried to scream above the screaming.

In a few minutes, I was in the principal's office. I tried to explain what had happened, but no one believed me.

"Mrs. Tutti called the school this morning,

Sam," said Mr. Davidson. "She says you've been stalking poor Carla."

Stalking?!

"You know what I mean, Sam," he went on. "Following her home. Bugging her all the time."

"I wasn't stalking anybody! I threw a snowball at her – one day! And I didn't mean to slide into her. It was an accident!" I told him.

But nobody listened. And for punishment, I had to report to the gym after school. I had to help fix up the gym for the Valentine's Day dance.

So at 3:30, I was in the gym with a bunch of morons. I was cutting out some stupid hearts and making stupid paper chains. And Carla was there, of course. She was up on a ladder, hanging stuff.

Then I got one of my more brilliant ideas. I decided to apologize to her in front of everyone. So I walked over toward her. But as I got near, this loser stuck his foot out. I tripped and crashed into the ladder. Carla flew through the air.

She didn't land hard. She wasn't even crying. Still, there was a lot of yelling and screaming from the teachers. I got sent to the principal's office again. I tried to explain, but nobody listened. And when I got sent home, I tried to explain, but nobody listened. My parents yelled a bit, then sent me to my room.

There was one person I hadn't explained things to. Simon. I know he's a jerk, but he is . . . *was* . . . my best friend. And he saved my life a couple of times in the last couple of years. So I wrote him a note in our Bat code. In Bat code, all the words are written backwards and the vowels get changed – AEIOUY becomes YUOIEA. Anyhow, the note looked like this.

Nimos. M'o arris. Lly stnudoccy. Ll'o noylpxu.

I gave Ellen a dollar to take the note to Simon. She was back in a few minutes. Here's what Simon wrote.

Tugrif to, rusil.

"You owe me a dollar," said Ellen. "Simon said he wasn't paying me to take this to you."

Forget it, loser.

Simon, I'm sorry. All accidents. I'll explain.

Well, wasn't that great! So Simon really wasn't my friend anymore. Fine! Who needed him?

The next day was really bad. All the guys made fun of me. I had to eat lunch by myself in the classroom. I wasn't allowed out for recess. And I had a detention after school.

I was walking home about four o'clock. No other kids were in sight. Then I turned the corner onto Park Street and saw Carla up ahead. I'd know that dopey pink hat anywhere. I don't know what came over me. I just thought I'd give it one more try.

"Carla! Hey, Carla!" I yelled. She turned around, saw me and started running. "Hey! Wait up! I'm sorry!"

She stopped, scooped up some snow, then threw a snowball at me. Then she kept running.

A van pulled up beside her and honked. She waved to the driver and ran over to the van. Just before she hopped in, she thumbed her nose at me.

Well, that was that. I was finished trying to be nice. I went home, ate dinner and went up to my room.

And about nine o'clock, the phone rang. And about one minute later, my mom burst into my room. "Where's Carla?" she screamed.

"What?"

"Carla's missing! Where is she?"

I shook my head. "How would I know? Ask Simon."

And then there was a loud pounding at the door. My mom ran downstairs, then she shouted up for me.

The police were in our kitchen. And they were all looking at me.

Uh-oh.

CHAPTER THREE

Kidnapped!

It turned out that Carla didn't make it home after school. She didn't call home, either. Her mom phoned everybody, but no one knew where she was. But someone saw me walking behind her on Park Street. Mrs. Tutti called the cops, and now the cops were calling on me.

I tried explaining again.

"I never 'stalked' Carla," I said. "I never even

meant to hit her with that snowball or anything. Stuff just happened."

"Listen, son," said one of the cops. "You've hit her and knocked her down and – "

"Accidents!!!" I yelled.

"And she broke up your friendship with your best friend. Right?"

I squirmed. "Well, yeah. *That* part's right."

"So it seems only reasonable that you have something to do with her disappearance," said the cop. "You were the last person to see her."

My mom moaned. My dad said, "Out with it, son. What happened?"

I looked at my parents. "This is just great. Thanks for your trust. How could you think . . . ," I stopped talking. Another brainstorm!

"But I'm not the last person!" I yelled. "I saw her get into a car. No, it was a van. On Park Street."

"Are you lying, Sam? Be very careful," said the cop.

"I'm not lying. This van honked and she got in."

Suddenly the cops were really serious. "What kind of van?"

I tried to remember. "Well . . . it wasn't special. Just an old white van. I hardly remember."

So then the cops made me go over and over my story. What did the van look like? What time was it? Are you sure? Did you see the driver? Did you see the license plate? And on and on.

Well, it was just after five, and I didn't see the driver, and I didn't look at the plate. Why would I?

"But it had an awful lot of mud on it," I suddenly remembered.

"Mud? In this weather?" asked a cop.

I nodded.

Then a cop phoned Mrs. Tutti to ask about the van. And for a moment, we thought all was solved. Mrs. Tutti had a friend who drove an old white van. So some other cops went off to his house. But it didn't pan out. The guy was at the dentist all afternoon, so it wasn't him.

"But it might explain *why* Carla got in the van," said one of the cops. "She might have thought she knew the driver. And she *was* trying to get away from you, Sam."

Everybody looked at me again. What could I say?

The cops left and I tried to sleep. But the cops were back in the morning. And this time, one of them was Officer Brannon. What a relief! She knew both me and Simon. She knew all about the crooks we had caught over the last few years. She knew I wasn't a jerk.

"So, Sam, here's the deal," said Officer Brannon. "We've put out an Amber Alert for Carla. That means radio and TV stations are getting out the news. And it means we have cruisers looking for an old white van."

I couldn't eat my cereal. An Amber Alert is serious. I suddenly felt pretty sick.

"Now, what we're going to do is this," Officer Brannon went on. "We've got lots of police out, searching the streets. We want you to come with us. We're just going to drive around. Okay? All you have to do is keep your eyes open for the van. Okay?"

I nodded. I didn't think I had a choice. On the bright side, I got to miss school!

I got dressed and went with the police. And we drove around and around and around. Just up and down streets, looking into alleys, driving through parking lots.

I knew this was serious. So I tried my best. But after a few hours, I was really tired, and I was really hungry, and I really had to pee.

"Don't you guys have to stop for a donut?" I finally asked.

They didn't laugh. But they did stop. They pulled up to Pizza Palace.

"Is it okay if I run across the street?" I asked. "I really want Burger Bob's."

"Fine. Stay there and we'll pick you up after we get our pizza," said Officer Brannon.

I ran over to the hamburger joint. Should I pee first or order first? I went up to the counter and ordered two double burgers with the works, no pickle. Maybe I should make that three burgers. No telling how long I was going to be stuck riding around in the cop car. "And a super soda and a chocolate freezie twist," I added.

"That'll be fifteen dollars, fifty-nine cents."

I put my hand in my pocket. What an idiot! I didn't have any money!

"Hold my order! I'll be right back!" I ran outside and looked for the cops. I was working for them, right? They had to pay for my meal, right?

But they were still at Pizza Palace, so I turned to go back inside and explain.

And besides, I had to pee.

But that's when I saw it. The van. An old white van, splashed with mud.

CHAPTER FOUR

Decision Time!

A man got out of the van and went into the coffee shop. He didn't look evil. He looked middle aged, like my dad. A little fat. A little bald. Nothing scary.

I looked around for my cops. They were still across the street.

I followed the man into the shop. He ordered a coffee to go. Just my luck. Why didn't he order a muffin and sit down?

His coffee was ready and he started to pay.

I ran outside. Still no cops.

So I made up my mind. I ran to the van and got in.

I hopped the middle row of seats and lay down on the floor behind them. I saw some dirty towels covered with dog hair and I threw them over me. Boy, did they ever stink of dog!

For a couple of minutes, nothing happened. Then the van door opened and I held my breath.

The middle-aged guy started the van and drove us out of the parking lot.

Okay. I watch all those crime shows on TV. I knew I should pay attention to where we were going. Did we go left? Right? What street were we on?! This is harder than it looks when you're lying on a van floor that smells like dog. And I knew I was supposed to be listening for sounds – like train whistles or church bells – then I'd know where I was. Well, there were sounds all right.

The guy was slurping his coffee and going "ah" all the time. Then he burped. Then he turned on the radio. Country music! This was going to be painful. Then he started to sing along. Really painful.

Tears on my banjo-oooo
Cause I'm missin' you-uuuu.
Tears on my banjo-oooo
Who-uuuuu
knew-uuuu?

29

Oh this was awful! Could this get any worse?
And I still had to pee.

We drove for twenty minutes. Then we slowed down. He stopped the car and got out. Was this it? Would I find Carla now?

I lifted my head and looked. We were in another mall in front of another Pizza Palace. Did I have time to get out and call the cops? But what if the guy came back? What if he left before the cops showed up?

And sure enough, I saw him coming outside with a large pizza box. That was fast! He must have called ahead before I got in the van.

So I flattened myself on the floor again.

And off we drove, him singing away.

No sense talkin'
Now that I'm walkin'
Away from you-uuuuu
Headin' for the hills
Ain't payin' your bills

Cause you ain't bin
true-uuuuu.

At a stoplight, I made up my mind. I had made a mistake. This guy was no evil monster. He was just some old loser getting pizza for the family. And he owned a dog! How bad could he be?

I decided to introduce myself at the next red light. I'd just say, 'Hi. Sorry about this. Wrong car.' And get out. Maybe he would have a heart attack. Big deal. He'd get over it.

So I started to move. And then I saw something. Sticking out from under the seat.

A pink hat with hearts hanging off it.

CHAPTER FIVE

Rescue!

I froze.

I stopped breathing.

I didn't even have to pee anymore.

Could he hear it? My heart hammering in my chest?

Slowly, I settled back down on the floor. And I really did try to figure out where we were going. But my head was a mess. I couldn't think.

Then I started thinking about the time I fell into a grave and someone threw a dead body in on top of me. And just like that time, I wasn't having any fun. I mean, this kind of stuff is great at the movies, or when it happens to someone else. But when it's you in there with the crazy people, you won't be laughing.

I checked my watch. It was just after three o'clock. We drove for about two hours. He kept singing and every now and then he laughed out loud. Hmmm. Yes. This one's really sane, I thought.

My brain cleared a bit. I could tell we were away from the main roads. I couldn't hear any traffic. Then, 'cause I started to roll, I knew we were going up a hill. Then my brain really cleared. We were in the mountains! Two hours – exactly. We must be near the ski hills my dad takes me to. But just after I figured this out, the road got all rutted and I bounced up and down, up and down. I grabbed the blanket and covered my mouth to keep from crying out. Man! That was one smelly dog!

Then we stopped. He opened his door and got out. I could hear his boots crunching over snow. I sat up and peered through the window. We were in

front of a cabin. And we were in the middle of a forest. The man walked over to the wooden door and reached up to the top of the doorframe. He grabbed something and bent down to the door. The door swung open and light poured out.

As soon as he went inside, I jumped out of the van. I ran around to the side of the cabin, away from the window. And when I calmed down, I snuck over to look inside.

Carla was in the middle of the floor, tied to a chair.

I pulled my head back fast. Think! Think! I said to myself. What do I do?! Well, I knew what I had to do first. Pee! So I ran off into the woods to do my business. But . . . this part is embarrassing. Still, I have to tell you what I did. Why go in the bushes, I thought. Why not write my name in the snow? I've always wanted to try it. I thought I had enough pee to write my whole name if I'd wanted to. But I stuck with just Sam. Only for fun, I wrote it in bat code. MYS.

I was just getting back to my window when I heard the door open. I crouched low and waited.

The man got back in his car, turned and drove away.

I ran over to the door. It was locked. But I reached up and my fingers touched the key. It was one of those big and heavy iron keys. I guess that's why he didn't keep it in his pocket.

I turned the key and pushed the door.

And when Carla saw me, did she say, 'Sam! My hero!'? No, she did not. She screamed.

"Sam! Are you behind this? Get away from me!"

Scream! Scream! Scream!

I ran over and put my hand over her mouth.

"Shhhh!" I hissed. "I don't know where the guy went. We've got to get out of here."

Carla stopped screaming. "Why are you here, Sam? How did you get here?"

So I told her everything.

And then she told me everything.

"I thought I knew him. I thought he was my mom's friend. And I just wanted to get away from you. So I got into his car. How dumb is that?" she asked.

"Real dumb," I agreed.

Carla gave me a dirty look. "But I was so scared I didn't do anything. He made me get down on the floor and we drove and drove until we got here. Then he tied me to this chair."

"Did . . . did he . . . hurt you?" I asked.

"No. Nothing. He's pretty nice. But he's kind of weird. He keeps coming and going and telling me I'm not doing it right. I ask him what he means, but he says he can't tell me. That would ruin the whole thing."

"What whole thing?" I asked.

Carla shrugged. "I don't know. He just says maybe he picked the wrong kid."

"Doesn't make sense," I said. "But who cares? Let's get out of here."

I started to untie the knots around Carla. I was down on the floor, behind the chair, so I couldn't see the door. Carla screamed, and I looked up.

The door was open.

The kidnapper was back!

CHAPTER SIX

Unrescued!

I think a real hero is supposed to jump in front of the girl to save her.

But I'm not a real hero. I stayed on the ground behind Carla. I mean, she wasn't *my* girlfriend!

The man came into the room and smiled at the two of us. "This is great!" he said. "This is wonderful! Why didn't I think of this?" He rubbed his hands together. "Sam, you're really going to make this work."

The guy was starting to creep me out. It was like he'd been expecting me.

"So here's the deal. After you eat the pizza, I'm going to leave you two alone. And I want you to really go for it! Give it all you've got!"

Well, Carla was right. He was nice. Weird, but polite.

"Give it all we've got?" I asked.

He smiled. "Oh, Sam, I can't tell you. That wouldn't be right. It would spoil the whole thing." And he made that "tsk tsk" sound. "Now, who wants pizza before we start?"

"I'm not hungry," Carla muttered.

"I am," I said. "I'm starving."

Carla gave me a real dirty look.

"What?" I said, catching the look. "I've been out all day looking for you. I didn't even finish my cereal. And no lunch. So there!" I grabbed two slices of cold, soggy pizza.

"Want something to drink?" the man asked.

I nodded. But then I changed my mind. What if I had to pee again?

I finished eating and the man said, "Okay, Sam. Please take off your jacket and hat."

I took off my jacket and hat.

He looked at me. "And you're going to have to take off your sweatshirt, too."

"No way," I said.

Then he patted a bulge in his pocket. "I said . . ."

He didn't have to say anything else. I took off my hoodie.

"And your boots and socks."

This was just too weird. But I took off my boots and socks. I looked over at Carla and rolled my eyes. But then I realized that she was barefoot, too. I guess the guy didn't want us running off.

"This is as far as I go," I declared. Just in case he thought I was taking off any more!

The man shrugged. "And now, sit down. I have to tie you up."

So I said, "No way," again.

But he put his hand in his pocket again, so I sat down.

Like a weenie, I sat there while he tied me up.

He put my hands behind the back of the chair and tied the rope around me and the chair.

"Perfect!" he said. Then he smiled at us.

"Aren't you going to gag us?" I asked.

Carla glared at me. "Shut up!" she hissed.

"Good question, Sam. But no, I'm not going to gag you. I need you to talk. That's my problem. I need it exciting. Get it?"

Well, no, I didn't "get it", but he didn't seem to care.

"Okay, I'm off," he said. "Have fun. This is your big scene. Don't let me down."

He went back outside. I heard him start the car and drive away.

"Now what?" I asked Carla.

She didn't answer me. She was sniffling.

"Aw, come on," I said. "It's not so bad. We'll figure something out."

"So how about *you* figure something out, Sam," Carla said. "So far, your rescue has been a big flop."

She was right about that. So I looked all around the cabin. There were two old sofas and one small

kitchen table. And nothing else.

I bumpity-bumped my chair closer to Carla's. I turned so that we were back to back. "Maybe we can untie each other's hands."

And so we tried that for a while. But it didn't work. And besides, it was kind of like I was holding hands with a girl.

"There's got to be a way out of here!" I yelled.

"You know what, Sam?" said Carla really slowly.

"I think that's what he wants. I think he wants us to escape."

"Huh?"

"All that talk. 'This is your big scene. Go for it.' I think he means for us to figure out how to get out of here."

Well, it didn't make sense to me. But then I'm not a crazy middle-aged kidnapper. And besides, there was something else that suddenly didn't make sense to me.

"Carla?" I said. "He called me Sam. How did the guy know my name?"

CHAPTER SEVEN

Escape!

Carla bumpity-bumped her chair around to face me.

"You're right," she said. "I didn't call you Sam. Not while he was here. I screamed at you when you came in. But . . . ," she stopped talking. "But that would mean . . . that would mean he's watching us."

I shook my head. "I *saw* him drive away before. We just *heard* him drive away now. No way he's lurking around outside." To prove it, I bumped my chair over to the only window. "He's not out there. He's not spying on us."

Carla sat there frowning. "Earlier today, he left me alone for a while. Then he came back and said I wasn't scared enough. He said I was just sitting here like a dummy."

"Well, we know the guy is weird," I replied.

Carla shook her head. "That's not it. He knew, he *knew* that I hadn't moved around or cried. How did he know that?"

We stared at each other for a couple of seconds. Then we both looked around at the walls at the same time. "Are you thinking what I'm thinking?" I asked her.

"Cameras," she whispered.

Oh freak me out!

"We gotta get out of here," I said. And man, did I mean it! But there was nothing – nothing! – in this cabin to help us. Two couches, one table . . . and one drawer in the table! I turned my chair around until I could grab the drawer handle with my fingers and pull. Then I had to turn myself around to look.

"Eureka!" I yelled. I stared at the knife.

I suddenly had another brainstorm. I bent down and picked up the knife with my mouth. I bumped my way over to Carla.

"Trrr arrf," I told her.

"What?"

"*Trrr arrf*!!" I yelled.

She stared at me. "Oh! You want me to 'turn around'?"

I nodded. "Yfff."

So she turned around and I bent down and started see-sawing the knife through the ropes on her wrists. I thought about this. If I cut her, will everybody yell at me again? Maybe I should let her free me first. I thought about this. Nope. No way I'm letting Carla Tutti near me with a knife.

It took forever, but I finally cut through the rope. Not too much blood, either. And I'll say this for her – Carla didn't yell or cry. Not bad for a girl.

As soon as her hands were free, Carla untied herself and then untied me.

"Okay! Let's go!" I yelled. I ran to open the

door. It was freezing outside. And we were in T-shirts and bare feet. I slammed the door.

"Any bright ideas?" I asked.

She shook her head. "We could die if we go out there without coats."

I nodded. "So maybe we should wait. We're not tied up anymore. When he comes back, we'll jump him."

She shook her head. "You forgot. If the guy is watching us, he knows what we're doing."

I shivered. This was nuts. So I shook my fist in the air in all directions. Then I ran around the cabin screaming. Then I sat down. Think. Think. Think.

And I had another brainstorm. I started to tell Carla my plan, but she was smarter than me.

"Shhhh!" she said. "Whisper it in my ear."

Way smarter than me.

So this is what I whispered. "I have an idea. Not a great idea, but it might work for a bit. But when we start, we have to move fast. If he's watching us, he'll figure out what we're doing and he'll come back."

Carla nodded.

"I'm going to slice open four of the cushions on the sofas. We'll stick our arms and feet into them. Then we'll tie the others around our bodies. Then we're going to drag this table outside. You sit on it and I'll push. When we get to the hillside, I'll hop on. Maybe – *maybe* – it'll work like a sled and we can get down the mountain."

Carla nodded. Then she smiled at me. "I think you're brilliant!"

Got that? Carla Tutti thinks I'm *brilliant*! Wait till I tell Simon.

So that's what we did. We ran for the cushions and I slashed deep slits in them with the knife. We pulled two on like boots. Then we tied other cushions around our waists. Then we pushed our arms into four more. We got the table outside and flipped it over. It slid over the snow just like I thought. And as soon as we got to the steep part of the road, we hopped on. Whenever we stuck a bit, I got off and pushed till we were flying again.

We were wet and cold, but we suddenly got a case of the giggles.

Until we saw the car lights below us, climbing the mountain.

CHAPTER EIGHT

Giving Up

"Into the forest!" Carla yelled. "If it's him, he won't know how far we got. If it isn't him, we'll flag the driver down."

Good plan. But I could just picture the driver of a car, being jumped on by cushion monsters. We looked like abominable snowmen!

We hid under some droopy pine branches. I peered out and waited for the car. I could hear it coming closer and closer. And then it was right in front of us. And it was an old white van.

It went by slowly, and it started going more and more slowly the closer it got to the cabin. He was looking for us. And if he got out of his car, he'd see our tracks.

"Should we keep going?" Carla whispered.

"I don't know. He'll be at the cabin in a couple of minutes. He'll be coming back for us right away. I don't know what to do. If we start out, he'll catch up to us. If we stay here, he'll find us."

I kept thinking about him patting that bulge in his pocket. But I didn't say this to Carla.

So we sat under the tree, doing nothing. When we heard the car coming back, we did nothing. Sitting ducks, that's us.

He came down the hill pretty fast, and he didn't slow down when he went past. We could hear the van for a long time, and it didn't slow down once.

"Maybe he's done with us?" asked Carla. "Maybe he got his 'big scene' and could care less about us now?"

I shrugged, which isn't easy to do when you're wearing pillows. "We should keep going."

We got up and pulled our table back onto the road. But pretty soon, it was useless. Farther down the mountain, it was pouring rain. The road was just ruts filled with mud.

"Well, I just figured out why the van was so muddy," I said.

So we hobbled along, shivering and slipping in the mud.

Carla turned and looked back up the mountain. "I hate to say this, but maybe we should go back. We could die out here. At least in the cabin, we'd be a lot warmer."

Oh man. I didn't want to admit it, but she was right. After everything – I had found the van, found Carla, rescued Carla, escaped with Carla – now we had to go back. This is when the tough guy says, "I want my mommy."

But I nodded. "I think you're right. It'll take us twenty minutes to go back, and a lot longer to go down the mountain. And I don't know what we'll find at the bottom, I don't know if there's a store or a house or anything. So maybe we'll be stuck out all night."

I was really fed up. My plan had been great. But pillows only go so far in cold, snow, rain and mud. I shook my head. I felt like a loser.

Carla touched my arm. "It's not your fault. You were wonderful. Simon will be so proud of you."

Simon. I thought of my best friend. He couldn't call me a *rusil* ever again. I had saved his girlfriend – sort of. And you know what? I was glad. Carla wasn't so bad. Maybe Simon wasn't such a weenie after all.

We turned around and started back up the mountain.

It took a lot longer than we thought. But finally we stumbled into the clearing and tried the cabin door. It was unlocked. Then we waddled inside and tore off the stupid cushions.

"Sam! Look!" cried Carla.

She was pointing to a pile of clothes and boots. And on the floor were some sandwiches and some bottles of juice. What the . . . ?

We yanked off the cushions and pulled on our

clothes. We ran over to the food and then we saw the note.

Dear Carla and Sam,
You were great! I'll let you know how it all turns out. I owe you everything. Don't worry. Someone will find you soon.

Yours,
Eddie

Who knew what he was talking about? And who cared? We had food, we had clothes, we had . . . thunder? Thunder?! What *was* that loud noise? And what were all the lights, all of a sudden?

We ran outside to look.

CHAPTER NINE

Rescued Again

Two helicopters were flying over the mountain. They went one way, then the other, lights going all over the place. We jumped up and down. Did they see us? Did they?

I guessed not, because they suddenly took off. The silence was terrible.

Carla and I went back inside. We sat down on the mutilated sofas.

"They must have seen us," Carla said. "They must have."

I looked over at her. Uh-oh. I thought she was going to cry again.

"Of course they saw us!" I said. Maybe it was a lie, but so what? "Now, let's eat this food."

I gave her a sandwich and a juice and we sat and talked. I told her all about Simon, about how we met after grade two. And I told her about our secret Bat Gang and about all the crooks we had caught. I was just about to tell her about me in the graveyard and the dead body when she suddenly went, "Shhhh!"

I stopped talking and listened.

A car.

Oh, no! Not again.

"We have to hide!" I yelled.

"No! Shhhh!" Carla yelled back. "Listen!"

We listened.

"It's more than one car," said Carla. "Maybe they saw us! Maybe we're being rescued!"

I ran to the door and opened it. Carla was right. Three cop cars came chugging up the mountain.

The doors opened and lots of people jumped out. I saw Officer Brannon and then I saw Simon.

"Simon!" I yelled.

"Oh, Simon!" cried Carla. And she ran through the snow and hugged him.

He hugged her back. I tried not to look.

"Hey, buddy! How come you got to ride along with the cops?" I asked.

"They thought I might be able to help. That I might see something or figure something out,"

Simon answered. "And they were right. I did." And he started to laugh. I wanted to ask what he meant, but the cops were all over us. We went back inside the cabin, and they asked us a million questions. Carla and I talked and talked.

Finally, I couldn't stand it any longer. I had to know. "How did you find us? Who is Eddie?"

Officer Brannon explained. "Eddie Yankowski used to be a TV writer, but he got fired a week ago because his scripts were terrible. So he thought he'd come up with a new reality show. Eddie kidnapped Carla to see what she'd do. Then he got you, Sam, as a bonus. Eddie was doing a video of you two the whole time. He was watching from another cabin close by."

Carla shivered. "Gross."

I turned to watch the other cops punch holes in the walls and pull out wires.

"Is he going to jail?" I asked.

"Not sure. But he's going to be in a hospital for a long, long time," replied Officer Brannon.

"But how did you catch him?" Carla asked.

"After you two escaped, he e-mailed everything to the television station where he worked. They figured something was wrong pretty quickly and alerted us," Officer Brannon said.

"And he told you we were here?" I asked.

"No. He just kept saying 'up in the mountains.' So we looked for muddy roads and sort of pinpointed the area. Then we got out a couple of helicopters," said Officer Brannon.

"But how did you know it was this cabin?" I asked. "These mountains are full of cabins."

Officer Brannon smiled. "Simon. You want to tell him?"

Simon laughed. "That part was easy, Sam. You signed your name in the snow."

CHAPTER TEN

Who's a Weenie?

We got home after midnight. My parents hugged me and kept saying they loved me. Then they threatened to kill me. Parents!

I thought I wouldn't be able to sleep, but I was wrong. I conked right out.

I thought I wouldn't have to go to school the next day, but I was wrong. My mom woke me up and drove me.

It wasn't so bad at school. All the kids treated me like I was a hero. Hey! I *was* a hero.

65

And that night, Thursday night, Mrs. Tutti had us all over for dinner. There was me and Simon and our families, even my dumb sister. Mrs. Tutti couldn't stop hugging me and crying. Then she'd blow her nose and hug me some more. Then lots more of Carla's family showed up. Soon all her aunts and uncles and grandparents and cousins hugged me, too.

It was enough to make a guy barf.

Except one of the cousins was in grade six at a school a few blocks away. She sort of looked like Carla. And she was . . . well . . . she was sort of . . . okay. I mean she had hair . . . and stuff. And she smelled like . . . okay. And she smiled at me all the time. Her name was Maria.

"Are you all right Sam?" asked my mom. "Your face is red."

"I'm fine," I mumbled.

Maria giggled. My hands got sweaty. Simon just shook his head.

And then we turned on the TV for a report on the kidnapping. Officer Brannon explained the whole thing to a reporter. We saw lots of shots of me and Carla tied up and barefoot. Then we saw lots of shots of me and Carla running around wearing cushions!

This was bad! I groaned and put a cushion over my face.

But then, when all the rest of them were laughing, Maria sat down beside me.

"You're so cool, Sam," she whispered.

I know my face went red again. Good job I was wearing a cushion.

But let's get the rest of this story over with.

I didn't get to go to the hockey game. My dad's schedule at work changed. He decided to take my mom.

"It's Valentine's Day, Sam. And your mom is my sweetie," he said. I hate it when parents explain stuff like this. Too much information!

Since I had nothing better to do, I decided to go to the dance at school. And I sort of asked Maria to come with me. Not *with* me, of course, but she could come along. If she wanted to.

Anyhow, the dance wasn't too lame. Maria and I kind of had fun.

So call me a weenie.

I dare you.

Sharon Jennings is the author of more than twenty books for young people, including picture books and novels for middle-school students.

Sharon had already written three Bats books for another publisher when she decided to extend the series for High Interest Publishing. Her first Bat Gang novel for HIP was *Bats Past Midnight*, set on the first day of school. Her second novel in the series was *Bats in the Graveyard*, set at Halloween. *Jingle Bats* is a holiday book set in a shopping mall. *Batnapped* is a Valentine's Day adventure. *Bats on Break* will take the gang into March Break and a final *Bat Gang* book will conclude the school year.

Sharon says, "There is nothing I like to do more than write. I become the characters and live inside their story." In real life, Sharon Jennings balances her writing career with being a mother of two sons and a daughter. She lives in Toronto, Canada, but often visits schools across Canada and the United States. For more information, visit her website at <www.sharonjennings.ca>.